Marvellous Manners

Cowboys
Can Be
Kind

Timothy Knapman

Illustrated by Jimothy Oliver

QED Publishing

Cowboys should be **brave** and **true**,
for that is the cowboy way.

But Cowboy Jack was **not** like that...
...until one special day.

Way out West in the playground,
Jack rode his cowboy bike.

He said, "I'll go wherever **I want**,
and I'll pedal as fast as **I like!**"

He **didn't care** about honest folk,
who played like **good** girls and boys.

Without warning he'd **shoot** right past them –
and **scatter** their games and toys!

He took people's things without asking
and shouted, "**You can't catch me!**"

He **laughed** when he let go of Lily's balloon
and it got stuck in a tree.

Then the day came when Jack saw a puddle next to Eve in her **brand new dress**.

And he thought, **"I'd love to splash her!"**
And then – well, can you guess?

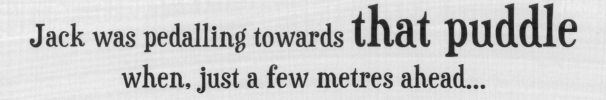

Jack was pedalling towards **that puddle**
when, just a few metres ahead...

...a **naughty** boy went cycling by,
and he splashed Jack **instead!**

Eve pointed at Jack, who was **dirty** and **wet**, and she gave him a piece of her mind.

"It **serves** you jolly well right," she said,
"for being so very **unkind!**"

"I never knew that it **felt** this **bad**," said Jack.
"I was **just** having fun!"

So he went round to everyone saying **sorry**
for all the **mean things** he'd done.

From then on Jack was **different**,
and did what a cowboy should.

He was **friendly** and joined in the games -
he was **kind** and **helpful** and **good**.

In no time at all he had plenty of **friends** -
he couldn't stop **smiling** all day.

There were races to run and swings to be swung
and so many **fun things** to **play!**

If you're ever way out West in the playground
and see Jack, I think that you'll find,
he's a cowboy who's **brave** and **true** -
he's a **cowboy who can be kind!**